At the Pet Shop

JENNIFER B. STITH

I wish for a fish at the pet shop.

A fish sat on a ship.

The fish are fed
a dash.

The fish rush to
the top.

Mom has cash for
a fish.

Get a fish with a
mesh net.

Set the fish in a dish.

Phonics Focus Words: Digraph sh

cash	fish	ship
dash	mesh	shop
dish	rush	wish

Decodable Words

at	Mom	sat
fed	net	set
get	on	top
in	pet	

High-Frequency Words

a	has	to
are	I	with
for	the	